The Boxcar Children Mysteries

THE MOVIE STAR MYSTERY

created by
GERTRUDE CHANDLER WARNER

Illustrated by Charles Tang

SCHOLASTIC INC.
New York Toronto London Auckland Sydney
Mexico City New Delhi Hong Kong

ISBN 0-590-68719-0

12 11 10 9 8 7 6 5 4 3 2 1   9/9 0 1 2 3 4/0

Printed in the U.S.A.   40
First Scholastic printing, March 1999

Contents

CHAPTER 1

Who's in This Old House?

"Smile and say cheese!" said six-year-old Benny Alden. He raised a camera and pointed it at his sister Violet.

Violet smiled. But she didn't say cheese. Instead she said, "Oh, Benny, you know that camera doesn't have any film in it."

Benny's elder brother, Henry, said, "That camera is so old it probably doesn't even work anymore."

"I know," said Benny. "I'm *pretending*."

Jessie stopped and raised her arm dramatically. "Cheese," she said to Benny.

"What are you pointing at?" Benny asked.

"I'm pretending I see a dinosaur," Jessie said. "Quick, take my picture."

Benny raised the camera. He pressed a button. "There! Now I have a picture of you *and* the dinosaur, Jessie."

The Aldens all laughed and their dog, Watch, wagged his tail.

The four Alden children were taking a hike through the woods near their hometown. They had once lived in an abandoned boxcar in these same woods. They had been orphans. They hadn't known that their grandfather, James Alden, was looking for them.

But then Grandfather Alden found them and took them to live with him in his big old white house on the edge of the town of Greenfield. He even moved the boxcar to a new place behind the house so that the four children could visit it whenever they wanted.

"There's an old barn up ahead," Henry said.

Jessie nodded. "And a clearing," she remembered. "We can have our picnic there."

Benny said, "I'm going to take some more pictures." Holding his camera tightly, he ran ahead of them.

The rest of the Aldens followed him up a steep hill. They'd almost reached the top when they heard voices.

"It doesn't matter where you hide the loot. Forget about it," a man's deep voice said impatiently.

"You'll be sorry you didn't take care of it," a second male voice said.

"Right now, I'm going to take care of you," the first man said.

Jessie, Henry, and Violet exchanged looks of amazement.

"Robbers?" whispered Violet in disbelief.

"It sounds that way," Jessie whispered back.

"Come on," said Henry, and led the way up the hill.

"It'll never work," said the second man. "You'll never pull it off."

"Oh, yeah?" said the first man. "I've done it before and I can do it again."

Just then, the Aldens saw Benny standing at the top of the hill. He was staring down in the direction of the voices and he wasn't even trying to hide.

"What if the robbers see Benny?" Violet gasped.

Without answering, Henry ran forward to grab his younger brother. But he wasn't fast enough. Suddenly Benny began to slip and slide down the hill toward the voices.

"Oh, no!" gasped Violet. She and Jessie quickly joined Henry at the top of the hill. They saw a short man with jet-black hair pulled back into a short ponytail, who was lying propped against the barn below. He wore faded jeans and a denim jacket and his eyes were hidden behind dark glasses. A taller man with a round stomach, chin-length brown hair, and a neatly trimmed, gray-streaked brown beard stood over him. He was dressed all in black and had a pair of dark glasses pushed up on his forehead.

The man on the ground said, "Go ahead, Stefan. Give it your best shot."

The tall man raised his arms.

As Benny reached the bottom of the hill, he said in a loud voice, "I have a camera, too, but it's not as big as yours."

At that moment, Watch barked and pulled his leash from Violet's hands. He ran down the hill and up to the man lying on the ground and began to lick his face.

Sitting up, the man began to laugh.

Henry, Violet, and Jessie ran down the hill after Watch and Benny.

"Wow," said the tall man, who was holding the camera. "What are all you kids doing out here in the middle of nowhere?"

"This isn't nowhere!" Benny said. "This is Greenfield."

"Greenfield," said the tall man. "Right."

"My name's Benny," Benny went on. "We're taking a hike. We live in Greenfield. That's my sister Violet. She's ten. And that's our dog, Watch. We don't know how old he is. We found him when we were living in the boxcar. We were orphans then, but we're not now."

"That's quite a story," said the man sitting on the ground. He was scratching

Watch's ears while Watch's tail wagged happily. He glanced at the tall man. "Sounds like a movie to me."

"It's not a movie. It's true," said Jessie.

"That's Jessie," Benny said. "She's my oldest sister. She's twelve. Henry is fourteen. He's the oldest." Benny raised his camera. "Can I take your picture, too?" he said to the man on the ground.

But both men threw up their hands as if to hide their faces. "No pictures, please," said the tall man.

The man on the ground cleared his throat. He said, "I'm Harper Woo. Everyone calls me Harpo. And this is — "

The tall man interrupted, "Smith. George." He smiled a little and said, "By all means, call me George."

Harpo gave George a look of surprise. Then he got up and began to brush grass and twigs from his pants.

"Why are you taking pictures of Harpo?" Jessie asked George.

"Uh . . . I'm in a photography class," said George.

"We're rehearsing for a play," said Harpo at the exact same moment. The two men exchanged glances. Then George cleared his throat and said, "For publicity. I'm a photography student and taking pictures of Harpo for publicity for a play he's in."

"Oh," said Violet. "I like plays. Is it going to be in Greenfield?"

"Greenfield," said George. "Sure. It's a nice, quiet town, isn't it?"

"Yes," said Henry. "Is the play going to be at the community center?"

"Sure," Harpo echoed George.

George put the camera into a bag and zipped it up. He hoisted the bag over his shoulder. "We'd better get going," he said to Harpo.

"What's the name of your play?" asked Jessie.

Bending over, Harpo picked up a big heavy leather satchel. "Nice to meet you kids," said Harpo as if he hadn't even heard Jessie's question. He and George walked quickly away through the underbrush and disappeared from sight.

"I hope it's a good play," said Benny.

"I don't think there *is* a play, Benny," said Jessie, with her hands on her hips. Her eyes narrowed. "The community center is closed for remodeling, remember?"

Henry nodded. "It's true."

Violet's eyes widened. "Do you think they were *lying*?" she asked.

"If they're lying," Benny said excitedly, "maybe they really *are* robbers. Let's follow them!"

"Yes," said Jessie. "I think you're right, Benny. Come on!"

Quickly, the children began to walk through the woods in the direction the two men had gone. Benny forgot about being hungry. Watch tugged at his leash, sniffing the ground.

Although they went as fast as they could, the Aldens couldn't find the two men. They crossed a stream and worked their way around a blackberry patch. They climbed over the trunk of a huge fallen tree and went up and down several more hills.

Finally they stopped at the top of a hill.

"Maybe, if we are very quiet, we can hear them walking in the woods ahead of us," Violet suggested.

So the Aldens and Watch stayed very still and listened hard. They didn't hear any footsteps, however. They only heard birds calling and the tree branches creaking in the wind.

Jessie sighed. "I guess we lost them."

"I think I've lost me," Benny said. "I don't know where we are!"

"Don't worry, Benny. I know where we are. I can see a road through the trees right over there," Henry said. "I'm pretty sure it's Old Farm Road."

"Let's have our picnic here," Violet said. "We can sit on this nice flat rock."

"Good idea," agreed Jessie. "And then we can follow the road home."

As the Aldens ate their lunch, they talked about the two mysterious men. They all agreed that they had never seen them around Greenfield before.

"And if they were from Greenfield, they would know the community center was closed now," Benny reminded everyone.

Henry took a bite of his cheese sandwich and chewed thoughtfully. Then he said, "They talked about hiding loot. We all heard them. That really does sound as if they had robbed a bank."

"Maybe, if they are bank robbers, their pictures are on wanted posters at the post office," Benny said.

"It's possible, Benny," said Jessie.

"The loot could have been in that big black leather bag Harpo was carrying," said Violet.

"But there haven't been any robberies around Greenfield," Jessie said. "Or even in Silver City."

"What I wonder is where George Smith could be taking photography lessons. They have classes at the community center sometimes, but not now," said Henry.

"When we heard them talking about loot, maybe they were just practicing the play," Violet said. "Maybe Harpo plays a bank robber in the play."

"If Harpo and George are telling the

truth, then why did they lie about the play being at the community center?" asked Jessie.

"If they aren't from around here, maybe they got it mixed up. Maybe they meant the community center over in Silver City," said Violet.

"But they wouldn't even tell us the name of the play," Jessie argued. "And you know why? Because there isn't a play."

"I think they are bank robbers and we should catch them and get a big reward," said Benny. He reached into the bag of chocolate chip cookies, then stopped. "Uh-oh," he said. "I ate the last cookie. How did that happen?" Benny held up the bag with a look of comic dismay on his face.

"I guess that's a mystery, too, Benny," Jessie teased him.

After cleaning up and making sure they hadn't left any litter, the Aldens walked down the hill onto Old Farm Road.

Henry pointed and said, "If we go that way, we'll come to the road that leads straight back into Greenfield."

"I don't think this road is used very much anymore, except by the farmers who live along it," Jessie said.

They began to walk along the grassy edge of the road. Benny held Jessie's hand. Violet looped Watch's leash around her wrist so he couldn't pull away. She didn't want him to run in front of a car.

But Jessie was right. Nobody used the old road very much anymore. The children didn't see a single car.

"Up ahead, just around this curve, is a mansion," Henry remembered aloud. "The Radley mansion. No one lives there now. It's been deserted for years."

"Is it haunted?" Violet asked.

Henry chuckled. "I don't think so. Not every deserted house is haunted, you know."

"I'm not afraid of ghosts," Benny said. "We even caught one once, don't forget."

Just then, Henry stopped and pointed. "Look," he said in a hushed voice. "The gates to the Radley mansion are open!"

"Did a ghost do that?" asked Benny, his voice getting squeaky with excitement.

"No," Henry answered. He paused, studying the rusted gates that had been pushed back to reveal a weed-covered, rutted driveway. He added, "At least, I don't think it was a ghost."

Just then they heard the sound of a motor. A truck came into view from the other direction. It slowed down in front of the open gates, then turned up the driveway and disappeared in a cloud of dust.

"That definitely wasn't a ghost," Jessie said. "That was a moving van."

The Aldens walked up to the open gate and peered down the driveway. They could see a long stretch of recently cut lawn. Curious, they walked a short distance up the drive past piles of branches beneath trees and recently trimmed shrubbery.

At the end of the curve in the driveway, they stopped.

"Look at the house," Violet said. "It's beautiful!"

The big old house sparkled in the afternoon sun, shiny with a fresh coat of white paint. Deep purple shutters, also newly painted, framed the windows. Purple was Violet's favorite color.

"I wonder who's moving in," Jessie said.

"Why don't we go ask," Henry said. "We can knock on the door and welcome them to Greenfield."

They started walking again. They didn't get far, however. A young woman appeared on the front porch of the house as the moving crew opened the back of the truck. She nodded and pointed at the open door behind her. She was dressed in black jeans, a black turtleneck sweater, and bright red sturdy sneakers. When she gestured with her hands, her short fingernails flashed red with nail polish that matched her sneakers. Her long, shining black hair was pulled back in a single braid and she had on a baseball cap.

Then she saw the Aldens and jumped from the top of the steps. She walked very quickly toward them.

"Hi," said Henry. "Welcome to — "

"Who are you?" the young woman demanded in an annoyed tone. "How did you get in here?"

"Through the gate. It was open," Benny said.

"Well, you can just turn around and walk right back out," she said. "Go on. Shoo."

"We just wanted to welcome you to — " Henry tried to speak again.

The woman folded her arms. "Go," she said, her brown eyes narrowing. "Now."

Without another word, the children walked down the driveway and back out to the road, with the woman silently following them. She slammed and locked the gates behind them. Then she walked back up the driveway.

"I don't like her," said Benny.

"Some people just aren't very friendly," said Violet. "Maybe the other people in the house are nicer."

"Maybe," said Henry. "But somehow I don't think we're going to get the chance to find out."

"Come on," said Jessie. "Let's go home."

As they walked away from the gates of the old Radley mansion, Benny looked back over his shoulder and made a face.

"I hope the house *is* haunted," he said. "Then they'll want us to come and catch the ghost and solve the mystery of where it came from."

"Oh, Benny," said Jessie. She laughed. "There's no ghost and no mystery, at least not at the Radley mansion."

But as she and the rest of the Alden family would soon find out, Jessie was wrong.

CHAPTER 2

They're Going to Rob That Bank!

"Don't forget my book about Jesse James," Benny told the librarian at the Greenfield Public Library the next day. "He was a famous bank robber, you know."

The librarian laughed. "I know. He and his brother, Frank. I used to like to read about them, too."

Benny said, "I can't read this book yet, at least not all of it. But Violet said she would help me."

"I will," said Violet. She smiled at the librarian and put the books she had just checked out into her backpack. The Aldens had come to the library early that morning to return books and check out new ones. Watch had stayed at home with the Aldens' housekeeper, Mrs. McGregor, because dogs weren't allowed in the library.

One of the reasons Benny wanted to go to the library was to learn more about bank robbers. "It might help me find clues," he explained.

As they walked out of the library, Jessie said, "Let's go to the post office."

"Why? Do you have a letter to mail?" asked Henry.

"No. But maybe we could look at the wanted posters," said Jessie.

Violet's eyes widened. "Do you really think we'll see a picture of George Smith or Harpo Woo on one of the posters?" she asked.

"We'll see Mr. Smith and Mr. Woo," Benny said.

"How do you know that, Benny?" asked Henry, smiling a little at his younger brother. "You haven't read any of your books about bank robbers yet."

Benny pointed. "Because they are right across the street by the bank."

The four Aldens stopped and stared. They saw two men, but the men weren't Harpo Woo and George Smith.

"Where, Benny?" asked Jessie.

"Right there," said Benny. "Those two men. They're in disguise."

Violet blinked in disbelief. Then she said, "You're right! That is George Smith and Harpo Woo."

Sure enough, at first the two men who stood outside the bank did not look much like the two men the Aldens had met the day before, but at a second glance it was clear who they were. George had his dark glasses on and today he had a hat pulled low on his forehead. He was wearing jeans, a colorful vest, and a turtleneck sweater, and his beard was no longer brown streaked with gray but jet-black.

Harpo's black hair had been tucked up under a broad-brimmed hat. He was wearing his dark glasses as he had the day before, but today he had a black goatee and long sideburns.

As the children watched, a short man in a windbreaker, new-looking jeans, and heavy black shoes walked briskly up to the two men. He was very tan and had silver hair slicked back. He, too, wore dark glasses. The two turned to him as he spoke.

The silver-haired man gestured and the two men looked warily around. The man who called himself George Smith nodded and pointed down the street, and the man in the new jeans walked on.

"Is he a bank robber, too?" Benny asked.

"I think he was just asking directions, Benny. Don't let them see us," said Henry, and pulled his sisters and brother back to stand in the shadow of a doorway.

As the Boxcar Children watched, George raised a camera and took a photograph of the building. Today he didn't have the big camera he had had the day before, but a small silver one. Harpo appeared to be talking to his own left hand.

"Harpo has a tape recorder," Violet said. "In his left hand. I wonder what he is recording."

As Harpo talked and George took photographs, they both kept glancing nervously up and down the street.

"Do you think they're planning to rob the bank?" Benny asked. "Maybe we should call the police!"

But before the Aldens could do anything, Harpo glanced down the street and seemed to freeze for a moment. Then he said something to George.

In response, George grabbed Harpo by the arm and pulled him into a blue van parked on the street near the bank. Then George jumped in the van himself, started it, and drove quickly away.

"Look! That must be what frightened George and Harpo," Violet said.

A police car had just turned the corner and was heading down Main Street toward the bank.

Instantly, Jessie jumped out onto the sidewalk and threw up her hand to flag the police car.

The officer rolled down her window and said, "Well, hello. What can I do for you?"

"We just saw bank robbers!" Benny blurted out.

Startled, the officer looked toward the bank.

"We didn't see anyone robbing the bank," Henry explained quickly. "We think we saw someone who is planning to rob the bank."

The Aldens told the officer what they'd seen and heard the day before and that morning in front of the bank. When they had finished, the officer smiled and nodded. "Thanks for the tip," she said. "We'll keep an eye on the bank."

Then she looked in the rearview mirror. "I'm holding up traffic here. I'd better move on." The officer pulled away from the curb.

Jessie put her hands on her hips. "She didn't believe us!" she exclaimed.

"No, I don't think she did," Henry agreed.

Violet didn't say anything. She was

watching the dark brown car behind the police car. The woman in the car had wild red hair tied back with an emerald-green scarf. Slashes of green eye shadow above her eyes matched the scarf.

As she drove by, she glared out her window at the Aldens, her face red with fury.

"Why is she so angry?" Violet said softly. "Why is she angry at us?"

"Who?" asked Henry.

"Her. The lady in the brown car," Violet said. But the brown car had already passed by and the other Aldens didn't see the angry woman in the green scarf.

Jessie turned toward Benny. "How did you recognize George and Harpo so quickly, Benny?" she asked.

"Harpo's feet," said Benny.

"You recognized his feet?" Henry asked.

"He had on the same shoes. Silver high-tops," said Benny.

"Oh." Jessie thought for a moment, then said, "You're right, Benny. That's very observant of you."

"I'm a detective," said Benny.

"You sure are," Henry agreed. "And it's a good thing, too. Because if the police don't believe us, we may have to catch the bank robbers ourselves."

"We can do it," Benny said.

"I hope so," Jessie said. "And I hope we can do it *before* they rob another bank."

"Let's go to the post office to look at wanted posters," Violet said.

"And then we can get some ice cream," Benny suggested.

"After we go to the post office," agreed Henry.

The Aldens went to the post office. But they didn't see George Smith's picture on any of the wanted posters, or Harpo's, either — even in disguise.

CHAPTER 3

Ice Cream and a Fire Alarm

"This is good ice cream," said Benny. "The best ice cream in the whole world."

"You always say that when we come to the ice-cream parlor," Violet said, smiling at Benny.

The Aldens were sitting at one of the little tables inside the shop eating ice-cream cones.

Just then, a tall boy walked into the ice-cream parlor. He was wearing a baseball cap pulled low on his forehead and he had on dark glasses.

"Lots of people are wearing dark glasses today," observed Henry. "And it's not even very sunny."

"The bank robbers had them on for disguises," said Jessie. She stopped eating her ice-cream cone. She stared at the boy in the baseball cap as he walked up to the counter.

A man stopped in the doorway of the shop. "Ta . . . Jonathan," he said. "We should be going."

"In a minute," said the boy. "Do you want some ice cream?"

"It's the man with the silver hair. The one we saw earlier," Violet said in a low voice.

The man patted his trim stomach. "No, thanks. Have to watch my weight."

"Okay," said the boy called Jonathan. "I'll be right out."

The man nodded. "Courtney's gone to get the Jeep," he said, and disappeared.

Jessie kept staring at the boy. Her ice cream began to melt and drip down on her hand, but she didn't even seem to notice.

"Jessie," Henry said. "What is it?"

"I'm not sure," Jessie answered, without taking her gaze off the boy. He turned to look around the shop as he waited for his ice-cream cone. He gave them a little half smile, ducking his head and turning away again at the same time.

"He acts like he doesn't want us to look at him," Benny said. "And Jessie is staring. Grandfather says it is rude to stare."

Reluctantly Jessie turned her gaze away from the boy. "You're right, Benny," she said. "It's just that — "

But Jessie didn't get to finish her sentence.

A shattering alarm went off right over their heads.

"Fire!" the girl behind the ice-cream counter shouted. "Fire!" She turned and ran toward the back of the shop. At the same moment, a billow of black smoke poured into the front door of the ice-cream shop.

"The exit is in the back." Henry jumped to his feet and caught Benny by the hand. "This way!" he shouted. "Jessie, grab

Benny's hand. Violet, hold on to Jessie."

Henry quickly led the way to the back of the shop. A bright red EXIT sign could be seen through the smoke.

The boy stood frozen by the counter. As they went by, Violet reached out with her free hand and grabbed his arm. "Come on!" she said.

A moment later, they had followed the counter girl out of the back of the shop into the alley.

"Is everyone okay?" Henry asked.

"We're fine," said Jessie. "And we were the only ones in the shop."

"It's a good thing," said the counter girl. "If it had been busier, it could have been a disaster."

They were standing in the alley. "Fire trucks are coming," said Benny. "Listen."

They ran along the alley toward the street. As they reached the sidewalk, a woman with bright red hair ran forward. "Where is he?" she demanded.

"Who?" asked Jessie.

But the woman didn't answer. She pushed

past the Aldens, muttering under her breath.

"Jessie," said Violet. "That was the same woman who was behind the police officer before." Then Violet remembered the boy in the baseball cap. She looked around, too. But he was nowhere in sight.

Nearby, a firefighter was squirting foam on a trash can while a small crowd stood and watched.

"What happened?" asked Benny.

"A fire in the trash can," the firefighter said. She shook her head. "We're not sure how it happened, but it looks like someone tried to create a lot of smoke deliberately."

Another firefighter emerged from the ice-cream parlor. "Everything's okay inside," he said. "No fire there. But the trash can shouldn't have been so near the door. Someone must have moved it. The smoke is what set off the alarm."

"If I didn't know better," the first firefighter said, "I'd say someone was trying to smoke out the people in the ice-cream parlor."

The counter girl said, "I told everybody

to leave the moment the alarm went off. We left by the rear exit."

"She didn't tell us to leave," Benny said indignantly. "She just ran out!"

But the firefighter didn't hear Benny's protest. She was nodding at the girl approvingly. "That's what you should do," said the firefighter. "When there is a fire alarm, don't wait. Leave as quickly and calmly as possible."

Henry saw a photographer from the local newspaper begin to take pictures of the firefighters and the front of the ice-cream shop. As he did, the reporter who was with him stepped up to speak to the girl who worked there. "Yes," the Aldens heard her say. "The moment I heard the alarm, I showed everybody the way to the exit and told them to leave. That's what you're supposed to do. I guess that makes me a hero."

"You're the hero, Henry," said Jessie. "You helped us all get out of the ice-cream parlor."

"Well, I guess it's time for us to go home, anyway," Henry said.

They got their bicycles and began to walk down Main Street toward home.

Violet stopped and pointed. "There he is. The boy who was in the ice-cream shop."

They stood and watched as a red Jeep turned the corner ahead. A young woman with her hair in a long dark braid was driving. The man with the silver hair sat in the backseat. And the boy in the baseball cap was slumped down in the front seat.

He looked unhappy.

"That woman," said Henry. "Don't you recognize her?"

"Yes!" cried Jessie. "She's the woman who was so rude to us at the old Radley place yesterday!"

CHAPTER 4

A New Friend for Watch

"Do any bank robbers live in Greenfield, Grandfather?" Benny asked at dinner that night.

James Alden finished putting mashed potatoes on his plate. Then he passed the potatoes to Henry. He looked at his youngest grandchild. "Not that I know of," he said. "Why do you ask?"

"Because we saw some bank robbers today," Benny said. "Outside the bank."

"You had an exciting day," said Grandfather. "First a smoke alarm in the ice-cream shop. And then bank robbers. Were they robbing the bank?" His eyes began to twinkle.

"No. We're not exactly sure they are bank robbers," Violet said.

"But they had disguises on," Jessie said. "And they were acting very suspiciously."

"How did you know they were in disguise?" Grandfather asked.

"Because we saw them yesterday, too, when we were hiking in the woods," Henry said.

He went on to tell Grandfather Alden everything that had happened. When Henry finished, Grandfather said, "It sounds as if you've got a mystery on your hands."

"And a haunted house, too, maybe," said Benny.

"A haunted house?" Grandfather said.

"The Radley house out on Old Farm Road," Henry said. "We saw a moving van drive up to it. The lawn has been cut and the house has been painted, too."

Benny added, "And we met a mean lady, too. She made us go away."

"The Radley mansion's been abandoned for years and years," Grandfather said. "Old Mr. Radley's only child, Estella, left home when she was just a teenager. Even that was over twenty years ago. Mr. Radley died a few years after that, but no one ever came back to live in the house. I wonder if Estella finally sold it."

"I wonder if that was Estella who told us to go away," Jessie said.

"Could be," Grandfather said. "After she left, I don't remember that she ever became the famous movie star she'd dreamed of being. Maybe she's come home at last."

"Let's go visit tomorrow and find out," Benny said.

"Maybe we will, Benny," said Henry.

The next morning, the Aldens got on their bikes and rode out of town toward Old Farm Road. They pedaled slowly so that Watch could keep up with them. Henry held Watch's leash as they rode.

When they reached the Radley place, they stopped and stared. The gates were closed today. A big sign hung on one of the gates. It said, NO TRESPASSING.

"How are we going to find out if Estella Radley is back now?" Violet said.

Just then, Watch ran around to the other side of the bicycle and got his leash tangled around Henry's bike pedal. Bending over, Henry unclipped Watch's leash so he could unwind it.

Watch ran straight up the driveway toward the gate.

"Watch, stop!" Jessie cried. "No trespassing!"

But Watch couldn't read the sign. He kept running. He wriggled through the iron bars of the gate and disappeared around the curve of the driveway beyond the gate.

"Oh, no!" said Henry. The Aldens quickly propped their bikes against some nearby trees and hurried after Watch.

"Watch, come back!" Violet called through the gate.

"Here, Watch. Here, boy!" Henry called.

Jessie whistled loudly.

Watch didn't come back.

Benny pushed the gate open and walked right through.

"Benny! What are you doing?" Violet exclaimed.

"The gate wasn't locked," Benny said. "I'm going to get Watch."

He, too, disappeared around the curve of the long driveway.

"Come on, then," Henry said, and led the way as they all followed Benny. As they rounded the bend in the driveway, they heard the sound of laughter.

"Look," said Jessie.

Watch was tugging on a stick. At the other end of the stick was an enormous shaggy brown dog. A boy not much older than Henry stood nearby, grinning.

When he saw the Aldens, he waved. "Is this your dog?" he called.

"Yes," Henry answered.

"His name's Watch," said Benny. "What's your dog's name?"

"Her name is Greta," the boy said. "Greta Garbo, after the movie star."

"Oh," said Benny. He didn't know who

the boy was talking about. "She's a pretty dog."

"I found her when I was in Sweden working on a . . . visiting, I mean. Greta Garbo was from Sweden, too," the boy said.

"Oh," said Benny again, still not sure who Greta Garbo was.

Suddenly Watch jerked the stick free from Greta and ran with it. Greta gave a short, surprised bark, then raced after Watch.

"They really like each other," the boy observed. By now the Aldens had gotten close enough to see him clearly.

Violet said, "You're the boy from the ice-cream shop!" She put one hand over her mouth in surprise.

The boy raised his eyebrows. He wasn't wearing his cap and dark glasses today. They could see that he was older than he had looked at first. He had black hair and blue eyes and long black eyelashes. He was wearing baggy jeans and an old sweatshirt.

"And you're my rescuers," the boy said. "I wanted to stay and thank you, but I had to leave. My name is, uh, Jonathan."

"We're the Aldens," Henry said, and introduced everyone.

"Is your last name Radley? Have you moved here?" Benny asked.

"Not exactly," Jonathan said vaguely. "Do you guys live near here?"

"We live in Greenfield," Jessie said.

"That's the nearest town, right?" Jonathan said.

"What are you children doing here?" a voice demanded sharply.

They all looked up to see the same young woman they had seen two days before. She had her hands on her hips and she was frowning ferociously.

"It's okay, Courtney," Jonathan said quickly.

"How did you get in?" Courtney demanded.

"Through the gate," Violet said. "Our dog wiggled through the bars and we came after him."

"I know you didn't wiggle through, too, so I guess it wasn't locked," Jonathan said.

Just then, Watch and Greta ran back toward them. Greta had the stick now. She raced up to Jonathan and dropped the stick at his feet.

Jonathan picked it up and Greta danced around him.

"She wants you to throw the stick," Jessie said.

"I know," said Jonathan, grinning. "I can speak dog, too."

Courtney came down the stairs and walked toward the Aldens. She was wearing a one-piece jumpsuit over a turtleneck sweater. She looked strong and almost menacing.

"It's okay," Jonathan said, sounding a little impatient. To the Aldens he said, "This is Courtney Foote. She's a little . . . protective."

"It's my job," Courtney said, her eyes never leaving the Aldens. To the Aldens she said, "I'll walk you back to the gate."

"Greta and I will come, too," said Jonathan. He seemed to be trying to make up for Courtney's rudeness.

"That's not necessary," Courtney said.

Jonathan gave her a sweet smile. Jessie stared at him. "Yes, it is," he said. He talked politely to the Aldens as he walked with them to the gate, but Courtney didn't say a word.

She opened the gate and stepped back, motioning for the Aldens to go through it. Henry bent down and clipped the leash back on Watch's collar.

"Come see me and Greta again," Jonathan said.

"We will," agreed Henry.

Courtney clanged the gate shut. She said in a loud voice, "We're having a lock installed on that gate this afternoon. We've had enough trouble."

Jonathan winked at the Aldens. "I'll know when I see Watch that you're here," he said.

"You should go back to the house," said Courtney. "For your own safety."

Jonathan shrugged and rolled his eyes. But he didn't argue. He and Greta began to walk up the driveway.

Courtney stayed by the gate, her arms

folded, watching as the Aldens pedaled away.

"Whew!" said Henry. "She really doesn't want us around."

"Who does she think is going to hurt Jonathan?" Violet wondered.

"Good question," Jessie said. She pedaled in silence for a little while, then added, "This is going to sound a little weird, maybe, but I think I've seen Jonathan before."

"Sure you have," said Benny. "At the ice-cream shop yesterday."

"No. I'd seen him before that," said Jessie.

"I think I have, too," said Henry. "And not on a wanted poster at the post office."

"But not around Greenfield," Violet said.

"No," Henry said. "Not around Green-field."

"We've traveled a lot," Violet said. "Maybe you saw him on one of our trips."

"Maybe," said Henry. "But I don't think so."

"He's very handsome," said Jessie.

"He is?" said Benny. "I liked Greta. I thought she was handsome. So did Watch."

"Oh, Benny," said Jessie, shaking her head and laughing.

Violet said, "Jonathan never told us his last name, or if he and his family had moved into the mansion. So we still haven't solved that mystery."

"We have lots of mysteries," Benny said happily. "Bank robbers and who lives in that old house and why that mean lady acts so weird and why Jessie thinks Jonathan is handsome."

Jessie blushed a little. Violet said, "Jessie's right. Jonathan is handsome. Like a movie star."

"That's it!" Jessie exclaimed.

"What?" said Violet.

"Come on," Jessie said. "I'll show you!"

CHAPTER 5

The Movie Star in Disguise

"Why are we going into the grocery store, Jessie?" Henry asked.

"You'll see," Jessie answered mysteriously. She led the way to the magazine section and stopped. She studied the rows of magazines, then reached out and picked up a magazine called *True Star Stories*. On the front of the magazine was a big, slightly blurred photograph of a star with his face half hidden by sunglasses and a cap pulled low over his face. Beneath the photograph in big black letters the caption read "Tate's Last Date?????"

Jessie walked back toward the front of the store.

"You're not going to buy that magazine, are you?" Henry said in astonishment.

"Yes, I am," Jessie said.

"But those stories aren't really true. They're just gossip and exaggerations, to try to make you buy the magazine," Henry said.

"Junk," said Benny, repeating a word he had heard Grandfather Alden say.

"Junk or no junk, it's going to help us solve at least one of our mysteries," Jessie insisted. She paid for the magazine and went back outside, where Watch was waiting patiently by the bicycles. She sat down next to Watch on the grass and the others gathered around her.

"Does this picture remind you of anyone?" Jessie asked.

They all studied the picture.

"Well . . . " Violet began, then stopped.

"It reminds me of Jonathan," said Jessie.

She opened the magazine and read the story inside. According to the report, the

movie star Tate Radison had last been seen at a movie premiere with an actress in Hollywood two weeks before. After the date, he'd just disappeared from sight.

Henry read aloud over Jessie's shoulder, " 'Tate was supposed to begin a new film this month. But where is he? Has the bad luck curse that haunted his last movie caused him to disappear?' "

"Bad luck curse?" Violet said. "What does that mean?"

Since Jessie had skipped ahead, she was ready with an answer. She said, "According to this article, Tate's trailer on the movie set got flooded; a wall of fake bricks, which were fortunately made of lightweight foam, collapsed without warning and delayed filming; and then a whole canister of film just disappeared."

"Why didn't they just buy a new can, then?" Benny asked.

"Canister," Jessie said. "And they couldn't because the film inside the canister was film that already had pictures on it. They had to refilm several scenes, which delayed the film even more and made it even more expensive."

"And then Tate got bitten by a parrot who was costarring with him in the movie," said Violet, who'd skipped ahead to read the end of the story.

"I think Jonathan is Tate Radison," Jessie said.

She closed the magazine and they all studied the cover again. Finally Henry said, "Well, there's only one way to find out. We're going to pay another visit to Jonathan tomorrow morning."

"If Jonathan is Tate," Jessie said in a low voice as they turned onto Old Farm Road and rode their bicycles toward the Radley mansion the next morning, "maybe Courtney is his bodyguard. Lots of famous people have bodyguards."

"Especially famous people with bad luck curses," said Violet.

"Exactly," said Jessie.

At that moment, they heard the sound of a car approaching. Henry wound his fingers around Watch's leash so Watch couldn't run out into the road.

A blue van shot past them in a cloud of dust and gravel.

"That's the blue van we saw a couple of days ago," Henry said, blinking and rubbing his eyes to get the dust out. "The one that George and Harpo were driving."

"It looked like it," Violet agreed. "But what is it doing out here on Old Farm Road?"

"Maybe the robbers came back to hide their treasure near the barn in the woods," Benny said.

"I don't think so, Benny," Jessie said. "I don't think they've got any loot to hide yet. And why would they go back to hide loot in a place where witnesses have seen them?"

"Witnesses? You mean us?" Benny asked.

"Yes. We saw them by the barn and near the bank and we heard them talking about hiding loot. That makes us witnesses," Jessie said.

"That makes us witnesses *and* detectives," said Benny happily.

Violet stopped. "Look," she said.

They saw that the gate to the old Radley place was closed today and locked. For a moment, they didn't know how they were going to get in. Then Henry spotted an intercom system on one of the stone gateposts. He pressed the button.

After a long wait, someone said in a gruff voice, "Who is it?"

"The Aldens and their dog, Watch," said Henry. "We're here to see Jonathan and Greta."

Another long wait followed. Then the gruff voice said, "He's not seeing people right now. You'll have to leave."

Jessie wasn't about to give up so easily. She pressed the intercom again. "Please tell him we came to visit and that we'll be back again tomorrow."

"Oh, Jessie," Violet breathed. Violet was shy.

The gruff voice didn't answer, but as the Aldens turned to go, the intercom crackled to life again. "Wait!" a different voice said. "Come on in."

They heard a loud buzzing and then the gates swung slowly open.

After propping their bikes against a tree, the Aldens walked up the long driveway. Halfway to the house, they saw Jonathan coming toward them across the grass. Greta was bouncing along at his side.

"I'm glad you're here," Jonathan said. "I was getting really bored and so was Greta. Weren't you, girl?"

Greta flattened her ears and wagged her tail. Then she went down on her front forepaws to invite Watch to come play with her.

Henry unsnapped Watch's leash and he bounded forward happily.

Benny, who had been staring hard at Jonathan, suddenly blurted out, "Are you really Tate Radison?"

Jonathan looked surprised, then amused. "You caught me," he said.

"Your name isn't really Jonathan. It's Tate Radley. You're Estella Radley's son," said Jessie, just to make sure.

Shaking his head, the movie star said,

"My real name is Jonathan Tate Monroe. My screen name is Tate Radison. Everyone calls me Tate."

"If you are a real movie star, what are you doing out here?" Benny demanded.

Tate fished around in the pocket of his sweatshirt and pulled out an old tennis ball. He held it up. "Here, girl! Here, Watch!" he called to the two dogs. He threw the ball and the dogs chased it.

"This is my mother's place," Tate answered, watching the dogs run.

"Estella Radley," Violet said softly. When Tate looked over at her, she blushed a little.

"Right," he said. "My screen surname, Radison, is a sort of play on her last name, Radley. I'm surprised you know her name, though. She didn't think anybody would even remember she had once lived in Greenfield."

"Our grandfather did," Henry told Tate. "He said she left when she was a teenager, over twenty years ago, and never came back."

"She was going to be a star," Tate said. "She worked on stage and in film for a while. Then she met my father and got married and they had me. My father is a musician and now my mother manages my career."

"You still haven't told us why you are here," Jessie said.

"We're going to film my next movie here," Tate said.

Violet clasped her hands together in excitement. "Really?"

"Really," Tate said. "But it's a secret. Don't tell anyone."

"Why?" Benny asked.

Tate began to walk back toward the house. "Well, partly because of what happened on my last movie."

"The bad luck jinx," said Jessie.

"Right again," said Tate. He didn't seem surprised by what Jessie knew. He acted as if he were used to people knowing all about him.

They sat on the steps and took turns throwing the ball for Greta and Watch as

Tate told the rest of his story. Getting nipped by the parrot could have happened to anyone, he explained, and it wasn't really serious. And having one of the pipes burst and his trailer flood was inconvenient and messy, but also something that could have just been an accident.

"But when that wall collapsed and the canister of film disappeared, I began to get worried. Especially since that particular canister contained scenes in the film that involved only me. That's also when I began to realize that I was being followed," Tate said.

"Who was following you? A reporter?" Henry asked.

"I thought so at first. But if it had been a reporter, sooner or later he or she would have approached me. And it wasn't anyone trying to take sneaky photos of me, because none appeared in the press."

"That's why this is a big secret, then," Jessie said. "You don't want anyone following you here. And you don't want any more bad luck."

"I just want to do my job and enjoy being a kid," said Tate. He sighed. Then, as if pushing away the thought of bad luck, he jumped up.

"Let me show you around. It's a pretty cool old place," he said.

With the dogs romping along nearby, the Aldens and Tate walked around the old estate. Much of it was still overgrown by weeds and vines, and they saw people hammering and sawing and raking and planting. On one side of the house they stopped by a fountain that had been cleared and repaired. Fat fish swam lazily in a pool below the splashing water.

Greta and Watch stood at the edge of the pool, gazing intently at the fish. Then Watch stuck his whole head into the pool.

"Watch, be careful!" Violet cried.

But when Watch pulled his dripping head out with a comical expression on his face, everybody laughed.

"That's no way to catch a fish, Watch," Tate said. "Greta could have told you that."

"Tate?" a woman called from the back porch.

Tate looked up and waved. "Come on," he said to the Aldens. "I want you to meet my mom. My dad's traveling with the symphony."

"Call me Estella," the tall, slender woman insisted as she shook hands with each of the Aldens. She was as colorful as an exotic flower, in rose-colored pants, a wide sash of turquoise, and a loose shirt splashed with rose, turquoise, and yellow flowers and green leaves. Like Tate, she had jet-black hair and thick curling eyelashes, but her eyes were dark brown instead of blue.

When Benny shook hands with Estella, he said, "You look more like a movie star than Tate."

Estella laughed. "You'll go far, Benny," she said.

"I don't want to go anywhere," said Benny. "I like it in Greenfield."

Estella laughed again, throwing back her head.

"Estella? Telephone call for you. And we still need to finish going over that contract." The man with the silver hair came out of the house. Even though he had been inside, he had on sunglasses.

"This is Eddie Hampton," Tate said, and introduced the Aldens to his agent. "He's visiting."

"Briefly, briefly," said the agent. "Estella? That contract?"

"Have a nice visit to Greenfield," said Henry politely.

"Greenfield? Is that where I am? Who knew?" said Eddie, shaking his head. He was still shaking his head as he went back in the house.

Estella laughed and followed him. From the doorway, she fluttered her fingers at the Aldens. "Nice to meet you. See you soon, I hope," she said.

Jessie looked at her wristwatch. "Uh-oh," she said. "We have to go now to be home in time for lunch."

"I'll walk you to the gate and get the

mail," Tate said. "Next time, maybe you can stay for lunch."

"I'd like that," Benny said.

Courtney seemed to come from nowhere. "Don't go outside the gate," she said to Tate. She nodded at the Aldens. "Welcome back." Her voice was curt, but she didn't seem quite as unfriendly as she had the day before.

"Thank you," Violet said politely.

"See you in a minute, Court," Tate said.

"If not, I'll come looking for you," she warned.

When they were out of earshot of Courtney, Tate said, "This is her first bodyguard job for the major star of a picture. I've never had a bodyguard before, but the producers insisted on it after what happened last time."

"She seems very . . . tough," said Jessie.

"She is," Tate said. "And determined. She doesn't want anything to go wrong."

At the gate, he punched a code onto a keypad set behind a small door in the back of one of the stone gateposts. The gate swung slowly open. Henry knelt and snapped on Watch's leash.

As the Aldens walked out, Tate walked with them.

"Courtney told you to stay inside," Violet said in an alarmed voice.

Tate said, "I'm just going to get the mail out of the—"

"Who's there?" Jessie interrupted. She pointed as a shadowy figure darted out of the bushes across the road and into the deep cover of the woods beyond.

CHAPTER 6

A Mysterious Letter

Watch and Greta barked. Tate grabbed Greta's collar and Henry held on tightly to Watch's leash.

Jessie ran into the woods, but it was too late. Whoever it was had gotten too big a head start for her to catch up. Returning breathlessly, she said, "I couldn't see who it was."

"It was probably a reporter," said Tate. He didn't sound very concerned. He reached into the mailbox and took out a bundle of mail.

He drew out a single letter with the word *Tate* written on the front.

"Look," said Benny. "Your letter doesn't have a stamp on it."

"Or an address, either," Violet said.

"Looks like it was hand-delivered," said Tate, sounding a little uneasy now. Carefully, he opened the envelope and unfolded a single sheet of white paper. Printed in big black letters they saw:

Twinkle, twinkle, little star
The world will find out where you are.

Henry frowned. "What do you think that means? Is it some kind of a threat?"

"I don't know," said Tate. He turned the sheet of paper over, but nothing else was written on it.

Jessie glanced up the road in the direction that the mysterious figure hiding in the undergrowth had fled. "I think I know who delivered your letter," she said. "It was whoever was hiding in the bushes. Someone must have just put it into the mailbox when we came out."

"It doesn't make sense," Tate said. "If someone knows I'm here, what does he or she want?" He groaned. "I hope this isn't the beginning of more bad luck."

"Maybe someone wants you to pay money to keep it a secret," said Henry.

"There hasn't been a demand for money," Tate said.

"Don't worry," said Benny. "It's a mystery and we're very good at solving mysteries."

Tate smiled at Benny. "Thank you," he said.

"You're welcome," said Benny.

"One thing's for sure," Tate said as he walked back inside the gate. "I'm not going to tell Courtney about this. It would make her even more overprotective than she is now."

"Be careful, though," Jessie warned.

"I will," said Tate. He smiled and waved. "Come back tomorrow. We're still scouting locations for the movie and I don't have much to do right now."

"Okay," said Benny.

The Aldens wheeled their bikes back out onto the road. Jessie folded her jacket into the basket of her bike and gave Watch a ride in it. He was still panting from playing with Greta.

As soon as they got started, Watch stood up in the basket and uttered a short, high bark. At the same moment, Henry slowed his bike and pointed. "Do you see that?" he asked. "Over there? Tire tracks."

The Aldens stopped their bikes and went over to inspect the tracks.

"They weren't here this morning when we went by," said Violet.

"Let's see where they go," Benny said.

They followed the tracks to the edge of the woods and saw that branches and broken brush had been pulled over the tracks in an attempt to hide them. Pushing the branches aside, they saw that the tracks stopped just beyond where the children stood.

"No car now," remarked Jessie. "But I'm sure there was one here earlier."

"Maybe whoever sent Tate the letter left a car hidden here," Violet said. "Or maybe it *is* a reporter, spying on Tate."

"What if it was the bank robbers?" said Benny. "Maybe they had their van in here."

"But the van was leaving when we turned onto Old Farm Road. And the tracks weren't here," said Henry.

Benny looked stubborn. "Maybe they came back," he said.

"I guess they could have," said Jessie. "But why?"

"Maybe they're not bank robbers. Maybe they're spies," said Benny.

Henry chuckled. But Jessie frowned thoughtfully.

"Look at this," Henry said. He bent down and picked up a piece of a bright red feather. "I've never seen a bird with a feather like this around here."

"A cardinal?" suggested Benny. "Cardinals are red."

"But too small to have a feather that big," said Violet. "It's pretty."

"Maybe it's a clue," said Henry. He

slipped the feather into his pocket. "We'd better get going, or Mrs. McGregor will be worried."

"A red feather, a blue van, a funny letter, bank robbers, and spies," said Benny. "Those are a lot of mysteries."

Jessie said, "It seems like the more clues we find, the more mysterious everything gets."

When they buzzed the intercom at the Radley house the next day, Tate answered immediately. "Wait there," he said. "I'll be right out."

A few minutes later, an unfamiliar figure came hurrying down the driveway. He was wheeling a battered bicycle and Greta was walking alongside him. When he reached the gate, he stopped and put a leash on Greta. Then he punched in the code, pushed the gate open, and stepped out to join the Aldens.

"Tate?" said Violet in a puzzled voice.

The figure in front of them had frizzy brown hair and wore little wire-rimmed

glasses. He had on an enormous shirt and looked almost fat. Then Benny saw the blue eyes behind the glasses and said, "It is you. It's Tate."

Tate smiled. "Yep. It's a disguise. Not bad, huh?"

"If Greta wasn't with you, I wouldn't have guessed so quickly," Violet said.

"Why are you in disguise?" Jessie wanted to know.

"Because I want to go into Greenfield. This way, no one will recognize me," Tate explained.

"Where's Courtney?" asked Benny. "Did she say you could go?"

"She went with my mom to run some errands," Tate said. "This is a perfect time to slip away."

Henry looked up and down the road. But he didn't see any suspicious vans or anyone lurking in the trees. "Come on, then," he said. He grinned at Tate. "Let's go."

As they walked through the peaceful streets of Greenfield, the Aldens told Tate about the history of the town and about some of the mysteries they had solved there.

"That's the old train station," said Jessie. "Greenfield used to have lots of trains come through it."

"We found out about it when our boxcar got stolen," Jessie added.

"But you got it back?" Tate asked.

Benny said, "We sure did. We can solve *any* mystery. We even found some stolen rubies."

"Taken from the antique store over there," said Henry, pointing to a store with a sign that read ANTIQUE TREASURES, W. BELLOWS, PROPRIETOR.

"Wow," said Tate. "Greenfield only looks like a quiet little town. From the way you talk, I can tell that anything could happen."

Suddenly Violet stopped. "There they are!" she gasped.

"Who?" asked Henry.

"The robbers," Violet said. "I just saw them slip down the alley behind the bank!"

"Bank robbers?" Tate said, his eyes widening behind his glasses.

"Come on!" Jessie said. She hurried down

the sidewalk and stopped to peer around the corner. "I don't see them," she said.

"Let's go a little farther down the alley," Henry whispered. "We can hide behind those trash cans."

"This is great," said Tate. "Just like the movies!"

"Shhh!" said Benny, frowning at him.

As quietly as they could, they all walked down the alley. They crouched down and stayed close to the wall. When they got to the trash cans, they squatted down behind them.

"Pee-eew! It stinks," said Benny.

"It's the garbage, Benny," said Violet. "Pinch your nose together with your fingers."

"I just did," said Benny in a muffled voice.

Just then they heard footsteps.

"Shhh," Henry warned.

A familiar voice said, "Well, we can't shoot here. It would never work."

"George Smith," Violet breathed.

"You're wrong. This bank is perfect, from every angle," said the second voice.

"And Harper," Henry whispered.

"Harper?" said Tate.

"Shhh!" said Benny.

But Tate wasn't listening. He stood up!

Violet grabbed the sleeve of his sweat-shirt. "Tate. Be careful!" she said.

Tate smiled down at Violet. "Don't worry about me," he said. "I know how to handle these bank robbers."

With that, Tate began to walk down the alley toward the two men, leading Greta with him.

Henry jumped to his feet. So did everyone else. Watch began to pull Benny forward, after Greta.

"Harpo, Stefan, you've been caught," Tate said. "Will you surrender quietly?"

The Aldens watched in amazement as the two men spun around. They were in disguise again today, but Harpo had on his bright silver sneakers.

Harpo's eyebrows rose. He pushed up his

glasses and peered at Tate. Then he said, "Tate! What are you doing here?"

The man that the Aldens knew as George Smith, whom Tate had addressed as Stefan, put his hands on his hips. "A good question, Harpo. Tate, what *are* you doing here? What if someone sees you and recognizes you?"

By then the Aldens had reached Tate's side. Benny said, "You know the bank robbers?"

Stefan's thick brows went up. "Bank robbers? How do you know about the bank robbers? Tate, did you tell them?"

Laughing and shaking his head, Tate said, "No. They don't know anything about the plot of the movie. They think you and Harpo *are* bank robbers."

Harpo said, "I know you kids! We saw you in the woods, when we were scouting a location for the hideout."

Benny look confused.

Violet said in a faint voice, "Hideout?"

"Stefan, Harpo, allow me to introduce my friends the Aldens. Henry, Jessie, Violet, Benny, and Watch," Tate said.

Hearing his name, Watch wagged his tail.

"And these two gentlemen are Harpo Woo and Stefan Kirk. Harpo is locations director and Stefan is the director of my next movie, *Money in the Bank*."

Henry said, "We heard you talking about hiding loot in the woods and then we saw you in disguise watching the bank and we thought you were getting ready to rob it. But you're not bank robbers."

Harpo laughed. "No. I'm in charge of finding the best places to shoot scenes from the movie. We're in disguise because we don't want anyone to recognize us until we're finished picking locations."

"Why?" asked Jessie.

"It's much harder to get things done when people are crowding around, watching and asking questions," said Stefan crisply.

"That's Stefan's way of telling us to go away so he can get back to work," Tate said.

Stefan smiled a little, but he didn't disagree with Tate's words. Instead he said, "And I might remind you, Tate, that you don't want to be recognized, either. I thought you were trying to stay out of the spotlight after all the incidents that happened during the filming of your last movie."

"I am. But I'm in disguise, too," Tate said.

"As long as no one tells anyone where you are," Stefan said, giving the Aldens a hard look.

Benny frowned. Then he said, "We won't tell. We can keep secrets!"

"Good," said Stefan. He turned back toward the bank.

Harpo said, "See you when we get back to the house, Tate. Nice meeting you kids —again."

"Nice to meet you, too," said Violet politely.

The Aldens and Tate turned and walked out of the alley.

"I'm glad your friends aren't bank robbers," Benny told Tate.

Tate laughed. "Me, too," he said. Suddenly he stopped laughing. He frowned and looked around uneasily.

"What is it?" asked Jessie.

"I don't know," said Tate. "I just had the funniest feeling that someone was following me."

The Aldens all stopped and surveyed Main Street. But they didn't see anybody suspicious, just friends and neighbors going about their business.

"Who could be following you?" Henry asked. "Nobody even knows you're here."

Tate didn't answer Henry's question. Instead, he grabbed Henry's arm and said, "Oh, no! Quick. Hide me!"

CHAPTER 7

The Red Feather Clue

"Behind the bench," said Jessie, without asking questions. She took Greta's leash as Tate dove behind a bench in front of the ice-cream parlor. The Aldens all sat down on the bench and faced the street.

Without moving his lips, Henry said, "Who are you hiding from, Tate?"

"You'll see," Tate hissed back.

A moment later, a woman with red hair strode toward them. She was wearing a big white hat. A large red plume curled over one side of the hat and bobbed gently as she walked. Before reaching them, she stopped and peered into the ice-cream shop. Then she turned and looked across the street.

"Are you lost?" Jessie spoke up.

The woman turned back around and stared hard at the four Boxcar Children sitting on the bench. She looked at Greta and Watch, who were sitting in front of the bench. Her green eyes were sharp. Then she smiled.

"What cute dogs!" she said. "What are their names?"

Violet's eyebrows drew together in a frown.

"This is Watch," said Henry. "And this is—" Just then, he felt a finger poke him in the back. Henry paused. He knew that it was Tate who poked him. But why?

Then he realized what Tate wanted. Henry cleared his throat and said, "And this is Sally." He put his hand on Greta's head.

"Sally!" exclaimed Benny. "But—"

Jessie put a hand on Benny's arm and gave it a little squeeze.

The woman said, "Watch and . . . Sally?

Hmmm. I know a dog that looks a lot like Sally, but her name is Greta."

"You have a dog named Greta?" asked Jessie.

"No," said the woman. "I don't have a dog. I travel too much." Her smile faded and her eyes narrowed a little. "In fact, that's why I'm here in . . . Greenfield . . . now. I traveled all the way here from California to find a friend of mine."

"Does your friend live in Greenfield?" asked Violet.

"He doesn't live here, exactly. But maybe you've seen him. He's got blue eyes and black hair and he looks a lot like Tate Radison, the movie star."

Henry said, "No one who looks like that is around here now." It was true. With his glasses and his hat, Tate didn't look like himself.

The woman didn't look entirely convinced, but after a moment she nodded and stepped back. "Well, I have to be going. It's nice to meet you and your two lovely dogs." She strode off down the street.

The Aldens watched as she turned the corner.

"Don't move yet," Tate hissed. "She's very sneaky."

"Who is she?" asked Violet.

"I'll tell you in a minute," Tate whispered.

At that moment, the woman popped back around the corner. When she saw the Aldens still watching her, she waved and went back around the corner again.

"I think she's gone now," said Jessie.

Cautiously, Tate got up from his hiding place. He pushed his glasses into place on his nose and said, "Whew! That was a close call."

"Why don't you go down the alley behind the bank," Jessie suggested to Tate. "We'll get the bikes and meet you at the other end of it."

"Good idea," said Henry.

"I'll see you there," Tate said. He slipped out from behind the bench and almost ran to the alley.

A few minutes later, the Aldens and Tate

were on their way out of Greenfield back to Tate's house.

"Who was that lady?" asked Benny.

"That was Monica Tripe," Tate said. "She's a reporter for *True Star Stories*."

"She's the one who wrote that story about the bad luck jinx on your last movie," Jessie exclaimed.

"That's right. If it hadn't been for Monica, nobody would have paid any attention to what had happened," Tate said. "But she was *always* lurking around the movie set. That's how she found out about everything."

"She's looking for you now," Benny said. "And she knew Greta's real name. But we didn't tell her."

"I'm glad you didn't. That would have given me away for sure. But what I don't understand is how Monica knew to look for me in Greenfield. Hardly anyone knows where I am," Tate said.

"Stefan and Harpo know," said Violet.

"And your mother and your bodyguard," added Jessie.

"And your agent," Henry said. "Anybody else?"

Tate thought for a moment, then shook his head. "No. Even if there are other people working on the film who know where we are going to shoot it, they don't know I'm here yet. In fact, we told everyone that I was going to France for a vacation."

"Someone must have told her," said Violet.

"But who?" Tate said. "We were so careful not to let anyone know."

When they reached Tate's house, the Aldens said good-bye to Tate and Greta. As they pedaled up to the gates, they saw Courtney standing by one of the gateposts. She had her arms folded and her mouth set in a thin line.

"Uh-oh," said Benny. "She looks mad!"

Courtney said, "Well, there you are! Are you trying to make me lose my job?"

Tate looked startled. "No," he said.

"Well, I will, if anything happens to you," she said crossly. "Come inside. We've all been out looking everywhere for you."

"But I left a note," Tate protested.

"I didn't see any note," Courtney snapped. "We thought you might have been kidnapped. It wasn't until I noticed that the bike and Greta and her leash were gone that I was able to convince your mother to stop worrying."

Tate shrugged. "Okay, okay," he said. "I'm sorry. But I did leave a note. And nothing happened." He said to the Aldens, "Thanks. Greta and I had a great time."

As Tate and Greta walked in the gate, Violet said impulsively, "Why don't you come to dinner at our house tonight?"

"That's impossible," Courtney snapped. "The security risk is too high."

"I'd love to," Tate said, ignoring Courtney. "What time should I be there?"

"Seven o'clock. And you can come, too," Violet said, smiling shyly at Courtney.

"See you then," Tate said.

Courtney closed the gate and locked it. Tate took Courtney's arm as they walked up the driveway. "Don't worry," the Aldens heard him say to her. "If you're with me, what can happen?"

"What a good idea, Violet," said Jessie.

"Let's hurry home so we can tell Mrs. McGregor," Henry said.

"Yes. And we can ask her to make an extra-special dessert," Benny put in.

"Tate will be safe at our house, won't he?" asked Violet anxiously.

"Sure he will. We have Watch to stand guard," Benny said.

"A movie star for dinner!" exclaimed Mrs. McGregor. "Goodness gracious." Her eyes twinkled. "I'd better make a special dessert. What do you think, Benny?"

"Yes!" cried Benny. "Cake and ice cream and pie and—"

"I'll make a cake," Mrs. McGregor said. "Chocolate cake with buttercream frosting."

"Chocolate cake is my favorite," said Benny.

"Every cake is your favorite, Benny,"

teased Henry, smiling at his younger brother.

"Today it is chocolate cake," said Benny. "Mrs. McGregor's chocolate cake."

"Let's go pick some flowers," Violet suggested. "We can fill a vase with flowers to go on the table for dinner."

"That sounds great," said Jessie.

The Aldens went out into the yard to gather flowers for a bouquet for the dinner table. They gathered roses and the long stalks of a lacy fern.

Benny found the feather of a blue jay. "Let's put this in the flower arrangement, too," he suggested. "It's a pretty color."

"It will look nice with the pink roses," Violet said.

Jessie looked over at Henry. Henry's mouth had suddenly dropped open. "What is it, Henry?" she asked. "What's wrong?"

"The feather!" said Henry. "I'd forgotten about the feather. It's still in my pocket from yesterday."

Henry reached into his pocket and pulled

out the piece of red feather that the Aldens had found the day before near the car tracks by Old Farm Road.

Violet gasped. "The red feather. It's the same color as the one on Monica Tripe's hat!"

CHAPTER 8

Lights Out!

They all stared at the piece of red feather. Then Jessie said, "It must have been Monica who had a car hidden in the bushes by the side of the road. But why?"

"To spy on Tate," said Benny.

"She must suspect that he is at his mother's house," agreed Henry. "And she wants to write a story about it. But she can't until she has proof."

"Do you think she was the one who left the letter?" Violet said.

"I don't know," said Jessie. "I didn't see

whoever it was clearly enough to know."

Violet said, "She was there that day we saw Harpo and Stefan out in front of the bank. Remember when they jumped into their van and drove away so fast?"

Henry nodded. "And I remember you saying something about a lady in a green scarf."

"It was Monica Tripe," said Violet. "Maybe she wasn't angry with us like I thought. Maybe she was mad that Harpo and Stefan got away."

"Stefan and Harpo must have recognized her, too," said Jessie. "That's why they left in such a hurry, and not because of the police car!"

"Do you think she's behind all of Tate's bad luck?" said Violet.

"He did say she was always snooping around the set of his last movie," Jessie pointed out.

"Maybe she caused the bad luck so she could have a good story to write about," Henry said.

"I think it was Courtney," said Benny. "She's mean."

"Oh, Benny. She's just doing her job," Violet said. "She's supposed to protect Tate."

"Benny, you might be right," Jessie said thoughtfully. "If Tate isn't in danger, then he doesn't need Courtney. She'd be out of a job."

"And he did say that they hired her right after all those things went wrong on his other movie," Henry said. "Maybe she caused things to happen after they hired her."

"She could have sneaked out of the Radley place and put the letter in the mailbox," Violet said. "She could have just climbed over the fence."

Jessie nodded. "And maybe she's the one who told Monica where we were."

"Or maybe she and Monica are even working together," said Henry.

He stopped and held up the red feather. "But we don't have any proof."

"We'll find some new clues," Jessie said.

"Don't worry. We'll solve this mystery so that Tate can make his next movie without being afraid."

That evening, Courtney and Tate arrived at the Aldens' promptly at seven o'clock.

Benny answered the door. "Oh, good," he said. "I'm hungry."

Courtney smiled a little. But she stepped inside ahead of Tate and looked around. She walked to all the front windows and pulled down the shades. When they got to the dining room, she pulled the curtains closed in there.

Grandfather Alden looked surprised. "She's my bodyguard," Tate explained.

"Oh," said Grandfather.

Henry introduced Tate and Courtney to Grandfather and Mrs. McGregor. Courtney nodded. She said to Mrs. McGregor, "Does that door lead to the kitchen?"

Surprised, Mrs. McGregor nodded.

"And is there a back door?" Courtney asked.

"A kitchen door, yes," said Mrs. McGregor. "I'll show you." Courtney followed Mrs. McGregor into the kitchen.

A moment later Courtney returned. She said to Tate, "I think you should sit at the end of the room away from the window and near the door to the kitchen. That way you can make a quick exit out the back way if necessary."

Jessie looked from Courtney to Tate and back again. "Has something else happened?" she asked suspiciously.

Slowly Tate nodded.

"What?" asked Henry.

"A phone call," Tate said. "Courtney answered the phone."

"What kind of a phone call?" asked Violet.

"An anonymous phone call," Courtney said. "Someone with a disguised voice. I couldn't tell if it was a man or a woman. Whoever it was said, 'Tate, Tate, it's your fate. Come out and play or you will pay.' Then the person hung up."

"That sounds like a threat!" Henry said.

"Yes," said Courtney. "That's why I'm being so careful."

"But who knows where I am? And how did this person find out?" Tate cried in frustration. "We've been so careful."

"We'll just have to keep on being careful," Courtney said. "Extra careful."

Grandfather said, "Well, I think you're safe here. Why don't we sit down and enjoy Mrs. McGregor's excellent dinner."

It was a good dinner. Both Tate and Courtney seemed to relax a little as they ate the delicious food Mrs. McGregor had prepared. The Aldens told Tate and Courtney about mysteries they had solved. Tate told the Aldens about life as a movie star.

"It sounds like a lot of hard work," said Benny, wrinkling his nose.

"And not nearly as exciting as some of the mysteries you've solved," Tate answered.

"I think it would be fun to be a movie star," said Henry.

"I'd rather be the director," said Jessie. "Then I could be in charge of everything."

"You'd be good at that, Jessie," Grandfather said, smiling at his oldest granddaughter.

Suddenly Watch came running out of the kitchen, where he had been napping on his pillow by the stove. He was barking wildly.

"What is it, Watch? What is it, boy?" asked Benny.

Watch ran to the front door and started scratching at it. And at that moment, all the lights went out.

CHAPTER 9

A Movie Star Trap

"Somebody's outside the window," said Henry. He jumped toward the window and pulled the curtain back.

Jessie ran to join him and said, "Look!"

They saw a shadowy figure scuttling across the lawn.

Then Benny said, "I can see the lights in the neighbor's house."

"You're right, Benny. Only our lights seem to be off," said Grandfather. "Someone must have made them go off."

"Stay here," Courtney told Tate. "I'm going to check this out."

"We'll come with you," Henry said.

But it was too late to catch whoever had turned the lights off. By the time they got outside, the shadowy figure was nowhere to be seen.

Suddenly the lights in the house came back on. "Grandfather must have fixed the lights," said Henry.

"Look," said Violet. "Footprints." She pointed to the soft earth beneath the dining room window.

"Boot prints," said Courtney, kneeling to examine them. "Not much bigger than my own. They could belong to a man or a woman."

Suddenly Henry looked around with a frown. "Where's Jessie?" he asked.

At that moment, they heard Jessie call, "Stop! What are you doing?" and then saw a flash of light.

They ran around the corner of the house toward Jessie's voice.

"Jessie? Are you okay?" called Henry.

A woman's angry voice said, "It's only you!"

The Aldens and Courtney stopped. Jessie stood in front of them near the sidewalk. A brown car was parked at the curb. A woman with long red hair stood near the open door of the car, lit by the interior light. Jessie was holding her arm. The woman had a small camera in her other hand.

"Monica Tripe!" said Violet.

Courtney suddenly stepped back into the shadows. Benny looked around in surprise. It was almost as if she had become invisible.

"What's going on?" Henry demanded. "What are you doing here?"

Monica pulled her arm free of Jessie's grasp. "Just taking a few photographs of Greenfield," she said unconvincingly.

"At night? Here?" asked Violet in disbelief.

Jessie said, "You're the one who turned out our lights, aren't you?"

Monica stepped back with an angry toss of her head. "I did not. I don't have to make up my stories."

"What stories? What are you talking about?" asked Henry.

"Why did you take my photograph?" Jessie asked.

"I thought you were someone else," Monica muttered. "I saw the house go dark and then I heard someone running in this direction. I thought it was . . . the friend I've been looking for."

"Well, I'm not," said Jessie.

"Maybe not," said Monica. She edged toward her car. "But he's around here. I know it. And I'm going to find him, no matter what you or anyone does to stop me!"

With that, she jumped into her car, slammed the door, and drove away into the night.

Courtney said, "It's a good thing Tate didn't come outside. I'd better go see how he's doing."

She turned and went into the house as quickly and quietly as a cat.

"How did you know that Monica would be out in front of the house?" asked Henry as they walked back to the dining room.

"I didn't," said Jessie. "I just thought I heard something and went to check it out."

"Did she turn off the lights?" asked Benny.

Jessie shook her head. "I don't think so," she told him.

"Why not?" asked Henry.

"I know!" said Violet. "Did you see Monica's shoes? She wasn't wearing boots like the footprints we found. She was wearing high heels."

The Aldens went back inside the house. Jessie said, "We should tell Tate we saw Monica Tripe. But what if she and Courtney are working together?"

"I don't think they are," said Henry.

"Why not?" asked Violet. "Courtney has been around for everything that has happened. She was in town that day when the ice-cream parlor had the smoke alarm. She could have hidden the letter in the mailbox. And she's the one who got the mysterious phone call."

"But she didn't turn off our lights," Jessie

said. "There is no way she could have. She was inside the whole time."

"And it couldn't have been Monica. Not wearing those shoes. And she didn't have time to change," agreed Henry.

"Courtney didn't want Monica to see her," Benny said. "She backed up out of sight when she saw Monica."

"She knew Monica would recognize her as Tate's bodyguard," said Violet. "That's why."

"You're right," said Jessie slowly. "I don't think Courtney is behind all this."

"Then who is?" asked Benny. "Monica?"

"If it's Monica, she's not working alone. We have to find out who is helping her," said Henry.

"It has to be someone who knows Tate is here," said Violet. "And if it's not Courtney, that leaves four other people: Tate's mother; his agent, Eddie Hampton; Stefan; and Harpo."

"But which one?" asked Violet.

"I have an idea," said Jessie. They had

reached the house. She grinned. "Let's go inside and have some cake and I'll explain. Tate needs to hear this, too."

The letter carrier opened the mailbox and slipped the mail inside. Then he drove away.

Benny said, "We've been here all morning. And we haven't caught anybody yet."

"Be patient," Jessie whispered.

Benny yawned and leaned back against the tree. "Oh, okay," he said.

A few minutes later, he leaned forward again. "I hear a car," he whispered.

Watch gave a little whimper of excitement.

A brown car came into view on Old Farm Road. It drove past where the Boxcar Children were hiding in the woods and down the road.

"It looked like Monica's car," said Violet. "But it didn't stop. Why not?"

Her question was answered as the car drove back into view from the other direction. It slowed down and the Aldens could see the driver clearly, despite the bright green scarf that covered her hair and the huge dark glasses on her nose.

"Monica," said Henry.

Still moving slowly, the car passed them, rounded the curve, and then stopped. "She must be putting the car in the same hiding place as before. She'll be back," Jessie predicted.

Sure enough, they soon heard rapid footsteps on the road. Monica appeared, holding a white envelope in one hand. She had a camera around her neck. Looking nervously around, she approached the mailbox in front of the big gates of the Radley mansion. Quickly she opened the mailbox and shoved the envelope inside.

Then she hurried across the road to slip into the bushes and hide. She crouched behind a tree only a few yards from the Aldens.

Tate came to the gate, opened it, and walked out. He took out the envelope.

Monica raised her camera, waiting for a chance to get a perfect shot of Tate's outraged reaction.

But Tate didn't open the letter.

Instead he walked straight across the road to where Monica was hiding. Monica lowered her camera.

Tate stopped on the other side of the tree.

Monica's mouth dropped open in shock as Tate said, "Did you leave me this letter, Monica?"

"No! That is, I—I—" Monica began to stammer.

At that moment, the Aldens came out from their hiding places and surrounded Monica. "Yes," said Jessie. "Monica left that note. We saw her."

Monica's head jerked around. "You!" she gasped. "What are you doing here?"

Henry gave Monica a sweet smile. "Waiting for you," he said.

Tearing open the envelope, Tate took out a single sheet of paper. Black letters the same as on the previous note were printed on one side of the paper. "If you hide too long. You'll soon be gone," Tate read aloud. He gave Monica a cool look. "Is that a threat?"

"No!" Monica's cheeks turned bright red as she answered.

"It sounds like one to me," Violet said.

"Me, too," said Benny.

"Well, it's not!" Monica said. "Tate, you're a star. But if you keep hiding, your fans will forget about you. That's all."

"I have a right to a quiet, private vacation just like anybody else," said Tate. "And I would be glad to give out interviews and talk to reporters if they refused to report stories that weren't true or exaggerate things that happened in order to make a good story."

Monica lowered her eyes, and her cheeks grew even redder. "I—I don't do that," she said.

"Yes, you do," said Jessie.

"And now you're sending anonymous letters and setting fires and making anonymous phone calls and putting out the lights in our house," said Henry in disgust. "Just to make a good story."

"No!" Monica answered, startled. "I didn't do all that! I just left the letters to try to make Tate come out of hiding. That's all, I promise!"

"How did you know Tate was here?" asked Benny. "It was a secret."

"And why did you keep turning up wherever he was? How did you know to look in the ice-cream shop for him that day?" added Henry.

"Tips," Monica said. "I got secret information from someone."

"Who?" asked Tate.

Monica shook her head. She said, "I don't know. Most of the time they were phoned in to me. A husky voice would tell me where and when to find you. I couldn't even tell if it was a man or a woman."

The Aldens exchanged glances. This sounded like the anonymous caller who had spoken to Courtney.

Monica continued, "But the first tip — about where you were, Tate—came on this postcard." She took a postcard out of her camera bag and held it out.

The Aldens and Tate saw a picture of the Greenfield town square on the front. On the back, in square print, were the words, *Look here for Tate.*

"Whoever it was had to have bought the postcard here in Greenfield," said Jessie. "When did you get it in the mail?"

"Nine days ago," said Monica.

"So it had to have been mailed the week before," said Violet. She turned to Tate. "When did you get to Greenfield?"

"I've been here for seven days," said Tate. "But my mother and Eddie came ahead."

"Did Stefan and Harpo come with them, too?" asked Benny.

"They came with Courtney and me," said Tate.

Henry said, "Well, we know your mother didn't cause this mischief."

Tate nodded.

"It has to be Eddie Hampton, then, doesn't it?" cried Monica. "Wow. This will be a *great* story!"

"Wait just a minute," said Henry. "It won't be a story until we prove it was Eddie."

"How are you going to do that?" asked Monica.

Tate glanced around at the Aldens. "Oh, I think we'll all be able to prove it — and then you can have your story, Monica. Well, Aldens, what do we do now? I feel sure you have an idea for how to catch Eddie."

"We sure do!" said Henry.

CHAPTER 10

Caught in the Act

Dinner was almost over at the Radley mansion when the phone rang.

"I'll get it," said Tate. He picked up the phone and talked for a little while. Then he returned to the dinner table. Courtney, Stefan, Harpo, Estella, and Eddie looked up as he sat down.

Tate smiled. "It's all set. We're going to go take a look at the boxcar I was talking about tomorrow morning."

Stefan said, "It sounds like it could be a

good set location. Harpo and I will come with you and take a look."

"Be careful," Tate's mother said. "Don't let any bad luck happen."

"It won't," Tate said. "And even if it does, as long as Monica isn't there, who will ever know?"

Eddie finished his coffee and stood up. He yawned loudly. "Time for me to get some sleep," he said. He winked at Tate. "Good luck," he said.

"Thanks," said Tate. "You know what? I think tomorrow is going to be my lucky day."

Tate stood in the doorway of the red box-car in the Aldens' backyard.

"Good, good," said Stefan, peering through his camera. Harpo began to talk softly into his tape recorder.

Courtney stood nearby, her arms folded, watching. Benny, Violet, Watch, and Greta stood next to her.

Suddenly a brown car pulled up the driveway. The car door opened and Monica Tripe jumped out, holding her camera.

"I knew it!" she cried.

"Oh, no!" said Tate. "She's found us!"

Suddenly the boxcar began to rock back and forth. Tate grabbed the edge of the doorway to catch his balance.

Benny was watching. "Look at the wheels!" he shouted.

A stout rope was tied to the front and back wheels. It was pulled tight. . . .

The old boxcar rocked and jerked.

"Jump, Tate!" Benny shouted.

Monica raised her camera.

Tate leaped out of the boxcar to safety.

Courtney leaped forward — and sprinted past the boxcar and into the woods as Jessie and Henry came out, each holding on to the sleeve of Eddie Hampton.

"Let go of me!" he shouted angrily.

Courtney stepped in front of Eddie. "I don't think so, Eddie." She helped Jessie and Henry lead Eddie toward the others.

Monica kept snapping pictures.

"This is outrageous," Eddie said angrily.

"What do you think you're doing?"

"Catching the bad luck man," said Benny, folding his arms.

"Bad luck man? What are you talking about?" Eddie said.

"You're the one who's been responsible for all the bad luck that's happened to me recently," said Tate.

"That's not true!" Eddie said.

"If it's not true, what were you doing in the woods, pulling on that rope and trying to turn the boxcar over?" asked Jessie.

"I got here early . . . and I saw the rope and I went to investigate," Eddie said weakly. "Anybody could have left that rope there. Stefan. Or Harpo. Or Courtney . . . or Monica. She probably did it, for publicity."

"What?" squeaked Monica in outrage.

"No," said Henry. "You did it. We were awake and waiting before you got here this morning. We saw you do it."

"And you had to be the one who called Monica," said Jessie. "Because you were the only other person who knew about Tate coming to the boxcar this morning. We trapped you."

"A trap?" said Eddie. Drops of sweat popped out on his forehead. "You trapped me? Tate, how could you? After all I've done for you."

"You mean after all you've done *to* me," corrected Tate.

"You set Tate up," Henry said. "You tried to make him look as if he had a jinx on him."

"Why?" asked Violet.

Eddie looked around at the angry faces. He took a handkerchief out of his pocket and wiped his forehead. He said, "All publicity is good publicity, Tate. That's my motto. You know that."

"That's not true," said Jessie.

"Tate, listen to me," Eddie pleaded. "I was just doing my job. When all those other accidents happened during your last movie, and Monica did that bad luck jinx story, that's when I got the idea. I figured if strange things happened during this movie, it would be great publicity. Get everybody talking. . . ."

"So you started the fire in the trash can in front of the ice-cream parlor," said Violet. "And called Monica and told her that Tate was there."

"It was mostly smoke," said Eddie. "Never any danger. But what a great story it would have made! Only you got away before Monica could find you and take your picture."

"And you switched off the lights in our house when Tate and Courtney came for dinner," said Jessie.

"I had Monica waiting then, too. But you didn't come outside like you were supposed to," said Eddie. "How could I get you any publicity if you wouldn't even be seen in public?"

"That's not publicity," said Tate angrily. "And you're fired."

Eddie threw back his shoulders. "Fine," he snapped. "You're not the only star in the sky. There are plenty of other stars — bigger, better stars—who'd love to have Eddie Hampton as their agent."

"Maybe. Maybe not," said Monica. She snapped one last photograph. "Let's wait and see what happens when they read *my* exclusive story."

"This is the biggest car I've ever been in," said Benny.

"It's a limousine, Benny," Henry said.

Tate had sent a limousine to take the Boxcar Children to the special showing of his new movie at the Greenfield movie theater. He was ahead of them in another limousine.

The limousines stopped at the curb where a red carpet had been put down. The drivers sprang to open the doors of the cars. A crowd had gathered behind the velvet ropes on either side of the carpet.

"What do we do now?" asked Violet.

"Smile and wave like a movie star," said Jessie.

So they did.

The lights in the Greenfield movie theater came on as the final credits of the movie began to roll. The audience began to applaud.

"That was the best movie I ever saw," Violet said to Jessie.

"It was exciting," Jessie said.

"And exciting to be in it, too," Henry pointed out.

It was true. Benny, Henry, Jessie, Violet, and Watch had all been in Tate's new movie. They had been extras, standing in the crowd outside the bank as the robbers ran away.

"It's so cool," said Jessie. "Maybe someday I'll be a movie director."

"I'm going to be a star," said Benny. He paused, and then added, "Just like the boxcar." He pointed up on the screen.

There, in splendid color, was their boxcar, with the credits rolling in front of it.

Then Jessie gasped, "Look!"

Just before the screen went blank, the Aldens saw the words:

THE MAKERS OF THIS MOVIE WOULD LIKE TO THANK THE PEOPLE OF GREENFIELD FOR ALL THEIR HELP — ESPECIALLY HENRY, JESSIE, VIOLET, BENNY, AND, OF COURSE, WATCH.

GERTRUDE CHANDLER WARNER discovered when she was teaching that many readers who like an exciting story could find no books that were both easy and fun to read. She decided to try to meet this need, and her first book, *The Boxcar Children*, quickly proved she had succeeded.

Miss Warner drew on her own experiences to write the mystery. As a child she spent hours watching trains go by on the tracks opposite her family home. She often dreamed about what it would be like to set up housekeeping in a caboose or freight car — the situation the Alden children find themselves in.

When Miss Warner received requests for more adventures involving Henry, Jessie, Violet, and Benny Alden, she began additional stories. In each, she chose a special setting and introduced unusual or eccentric characters who liked the unpredictable.

While the mystery element is central to each of Miss Warner's books, she never thought of them as strictly juvenile mysteries. She liked to stress the Aldens' independence and resourcefulness and their solid New England devotion to using up and making do. The Aldens go about most of their adventures with as little adult supervision as possible — something else that delights young readers.

Miss Warner lived in Putnam, Connecticut, until her death in 1979. During her lifetime, she received hundreds of letters from girls and boys telling her how much they liked her books.